JB'S BIG DAY

JB's Big Day

Illustrated by Kela Matthews

Kela Matthews

Jameka McCullough

To my amazing son, I love you very much! You are my
inspiration in life. Thank you for being my son.

Today JB starts his first day of school.

His mom came into his room to wake him up.

She says, "Good morning little man, time to get up."

Little man was his nickname, his mother gave him when he was a baby.

JB was excited for his big day.

He got up real early and got dressed.

JB brushed his teeth and washed his face.

He asked, "Mommy can you help me brush my hair, please? She did.

Afterwards he tied his shoes and had a quick breakfast.

Now he was ready for his big day.

As he was walking to school with mommy,
JB was a little nervous.

JB got in the classroom and saw his seat, he paused.

His mother squeezed his hand and kissed his cheek.

She whispered to him "You will be ok; I am so proud of you."

JB smiled at her, gave her a hug, and kissed his mother goodbye.

Now he was ready for his big day.

About the Author

Jameka McCullough is new author of *Secrets of My Pain.* Her work is to inspire others. Her writing career started out with a book full of poems. She enjoys writing and giving people hope through these writings.

CPSIA information can be obtained
at www.ICGtesting.com
Printed in the USA
BVHW021734151121
621687BV00002B/25